Cold Little
Duck, Duck, Duck

by Lisa Westberg Peters

Pictures by Sam Williams

MACMILLAN
CHILDREN'S BOOKS

First published in the United States in 2000 by Greenwillow Books,
an imprint of HarperCollins*Publishers.*
First published in 2001 by Macmillan Children's Books
A division of Macmillan Publishers Limited
20 New Wharf Road, London N1 9RR
Basingstoke and Oxford
Associated companies worldwide
www.panmacmillan.com

ISBN 0 333 96055 6 (PB)

Text copyright © 2000 Lisa Westberg Peters
Illustrations copyright © 2000 Sam Williams
Moral rights asserted

5 7 9 8 6 4

A CIP catalogue record for this book is available from the British Library.

Printed in China

For Becky
—L. W. P.

For Linda—my spring in winter
—S. W.

One miserable
and frozen spring

A cold little
duck flew in

brisk
brisk brisk

Her pond was
stiff and white

creak creak creak

And her feet
froze to the ice

You're far
too early,
Duck, go

back

back

back

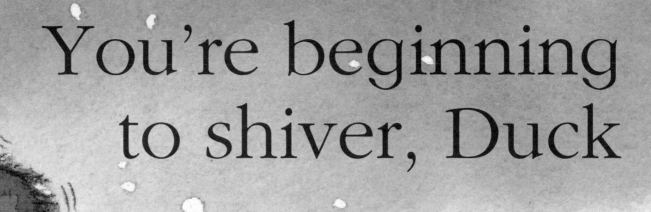

You're beginning
to shiver, Duck

shake

shake

shake

She tucked her
head into
her feathers to

wake

wake

wake

Her thoughts of spring and warmer weather

Of bubbly streams

and glassy puddles

drink   drink   drink

Of wiggly worms and shiny beetles

black   black   black

Of crocuses
and apple buds

pink

pink

pink

And blades of grass
in squishy mud

Her thoughts
of spring
filled the sky

Until a V
of ducks
flew by

flock

flock

flock

They saw
that spring
was in the air

blink blink blink

And quickly
spreading
everywhere

The ducks
flew down,
they dipped
and splashed

dunk
dunk
dunk

Come join us, Duck,
it's melting fast

The cold little
duck began
to slide

slick slick slick

Across the
disappearing ice

She wiggled
her tail,
waggled
her wings

The warm little duck
dived into spring

quack quack